SHADOW EYES 2

Where's my Child?

By

Tanya Hilson

Welcome Page

This page has been reserved for the welcome texts into the study about the book.

Copyright Page

Table of Content

Chapter One

The Private Detective Agency was elegantly furnished. Two desks occupied the common area, and one of its walls opened up to the kitchen. A 60-inch screen TV was mounted on one of the kitchen walls. Heaven Campbell, a Private Investigator, stood at the kitchen counter talking to Garrick.

"I see you like the chairs Nevaeh picked out," she said, watching Garrick lean into his black Vinsetto leather massage chair. Garrick was Heaven's Partner. Together, they ran Spotlight: A Private Investigation agency in Los Angeles.

Garrick tossed a small massage ball in the air and caught it. "I'll admit, they're different from the old worn-out chairs at the precinct." He walked over to the stainless-steel refrigerator shining brightly in the kitchen corner, opened it, grabbing a bottle of French Vanilla Creamer.

"I'm digging these black leather couches, too," he said.

Heaven opened four sugar packets and tipped them one after the other into her coffee. "Who would've thought we'll have a business together?"

Garrick smiled. "Ever since solving the murder of the mayor's daughter, it's like we became celebrities." He winked at Heaven.

"And we're going to keep it like that, Garrick."

"Keep it like what?"

Heaven glared at Garrick over the top of her cup. "You know exactly what I'm talking about. What happened between us will never happen again, so keep your winks to yourself."

"I'm with that," Garrick said. "Strictly professional."

The office phone started ringing. Heaven set down her coffee on the pale-colored yarn coaster and picked up the phone.

"Spotlight Private Investigators. Heaven speaking! How may I help you?"

Neveah's voice came through the line. "Hey, sis!"

"Hey girl, what's going on?"

"Turn on your TV. Turn to TMZ!"

Still holding the phone to her ear, Heaven grabbed the remote control off the desk and turned on the TV, flicking through the channels until she reached TMZ. "I see Devonte! "What did he do?"

"The cheating ass Nigga been traded to the LA Cougars!"

Heaven watched the clip of Devonte and his security detail walking through the crowded LAX airport as the paparazzi questioned him.

"Devonte! How does it feel going to another team after playing for the Atlanta Vipers for over five years?" A reporter asked him.

"Hey, don't get me wrong, I'm going to always love Atlanta and my teammates I played with, but I think it's time for me to move on. Hopefully, with my new organization and new team, I'll be able to get a ring."

"Is that the reason you asked to be traded? Because you have not made it to the championship with the Vipers?"

"The Vipers will always be a part of me, but money talks. All one hundred Million dollars." Devonte climbed into the black Escalade that was waiting on him.

Heaven shook her head. "You mean to tell me Devonte will be playing here in LA?"

"That's what I said when I saw this shit," Naveah replied.

Heaven smirked her lips as she listened on. "I see you're in your feelings."

An attractive woman entered the office looking stylish, dressed in a red Prada dress pants suit. Her long, silky blonde hair hung down her back to her waist. She held a black Prada Purse and wore matching black Red Bottoms, which clicked against the office floor as she walked. She looked to be in her forties. Garrick, who had returned to lounging in his massage chair, leaped up when he noticed her.

"Hey, sis! Let me call you back. Someone just walked into the office." Heaven hung up and walked over to the woman.

"Hi, Ma'am! I'm Heaven," extending her hand. "This is my partner Garrick. How may we help you?"

The woman shook Heaven's hand, looking around the office. Her purse dangled from the curve of her elbow.

"A friend of mine told me about the services you provide."

"Please, have a seat," Heaven gestured for the lady to sit at her desk.

The woman sat down, placing her Prada Purse on the leather chair next to her. Heaven could see she was nervous from how the woman rubbed her hands together. Garrick sat down at his desk and watched them.

"How may we help you?" Heaven asked brightly, trying to ease the woman's discomfort.

Garrick walked back to the coffee machine and poured himself another cup. "Would you like a cup of coffee, Ma'am?" he asked the woman.

"Please, call me Brook. And yes, I wouldn't mind a cup. Four creams and three sugars. Thanks for asking."

"You're Brook Amber of Amber construction," Heaven said.

Brook smiled. She was stunning when she did. Heaven noticed how even and white her teeth were. She reached for the cup Garrick had placed in front of her and took a small sip.

"Four creams and three sugars, as you requested." Garrick passes Brook, the cup of coffee.

"Heaven, you are correct. I am Brook Ambers of Ambers construction." She paused and took a sip of her coffee. "Before I tell you why I'm here, I want to know if this conversation will be 100% confidential." She was eyeing Garrick, who had walked back to his desk.

"Yes," Heaven said. "Whatever you say here stays in this room between you, me, and my partner. Your trust and confidentiality are our number one concern and priority."

Garrick walked back over to Brook and Heaven. "You mind if I take a seat here, Brook?

Brook moved her purse from the chair and placed it on her lap. "Garrick! Correct?" She looked over at Garrick, who had settled into the chair beside her.

"Yes, that's correct! And as my partner said, your trust and privacy are our first priority," he said with a reassuring smile.

Heaven leaned towards Brook and asked again, gently, "How may we help you, Brook?"

Brook, with a shaky breath, started speaking.

"As you may both know, my husband died in a car accident two years ago. Unfortunately, we never had children. I mean, we tried but found out my husband was sterile." Heaven saw that brook's eyes were starting to fill up with tears. She reached inside her drawer for a box of Kleenex and passed the box to her. Brook took out a Kleenex, folded it, and dabbed at her tears.

"I felt sorry for my husband when I found out he couldn't have children, but at the same time, I felt relieved because I did not want any children after what had happened."

"Brook, it's not wrong for you not to want children. That's your choice," Heaven replied.

Garrick stood up. "More coffee, Heaven?"

Heaven shook her head, still looking at Brook. "I'm good."

"Brook, would you like a refill?"

"Sure!" She offered up her empty cup to Garrick, who took it and walked back to the Coffee machine. He came back and placed the cup in front of her. She watched the steam swirl on top of the coffee.

"May I ask what you need our help with?" Heaven asked again.

"I don't know how to quite say this," Brook replied as she took a sip of the coffee.

"Start where you like," Heaven said to her. "We're here to listen, and again, anything said here stays here."

"There's a reason I did not want to have children. When I was younger, I was brought up in a polygamous environment. My father, regardless of how religious of a Mormon he says he was...." Brook paused and exhaled. "He was an abusive alcoholic." She scrunched up the Kleenex in her fist.

"I heard of the Mormon Culture but never really dealt with anyone who had experienced living that lifestyle," Garrick replied.

"Same here," Heaven said.

Brook smiled nervously. "Trust me! It's more than you could imagine."

"You walked in here for a reason," Heaven said, sitting up at her desk.

Brook stood up and started pacing the floor. Garrick and Heaven watched her curiously. Heaven tapped her fingers gently together, and Garrick leaned back into his chair and stroked his beard.

"When I was fourteen, my father forced me to marry a Sixty-Five-year-old man." Brook picked up her coffee off the table and then sat down. "Would you happen to have something a little stronger?" she asked Garrick. Garrick went to the cabinet and pulled out a Grey Goose VX Exclusive Edition bottle.

"Will Grey Goose be okay?"

Brook smiled at Garrick. "I see you know your Vodka. VX Exclusive is one of my favorite brands, and I wouldn't mind a double shot."

Garrick pulled out a rock glass.

"Would you like this neat or on the rocks?"

"Neat."

Garrick poured the drink and passed the glass to Brook. When she took it, he saw that her hands shook. She brought the glass up to her lips and took a large gulp.

"I'm just a little nervous," she said. "I'm about to tell you something I've never told anyone, not even my husband." She begins pacing the floor again.

Heaven pulled out a small notebook from her drawer. "Brook, do you mind if I take some notes of our conversation?"

Brook eyed the notebook nervously. Her shot glass was empty, and she had stopped pacing.

"Again, whatever you say here is strictly confidential," Heaven reassured her.

Brook went over to the cabinet and poured herself another glass of Vodka. Garrick and Heaven exchanged looks.

"You might want to tread light on that," Garrick said, "Especially if you're driving."

"I can hold my liquor."

"Still! I'm just saying, take it slow."

"I'm not driving. I have a chauffeur who takes me wherever I need to go. But, thanks for being concerned."

"To make you feel more comfortable, Brook, we can sign an NDA?" Heaven suggested.

"I'll take your word for it. Chief Williams and my husband were good friends before my husband's accident."

"Hmm, was Chief Williams the friend you were talking about when you said a friend referred you to us?" Garrick asked.

"Yes, that's correct! And I also followed the case of the Mayor's daughter.
After solving her murder, I see why you became Private Investigators."

Heaven opened the notebook.

"May we proceed to the reason why you're here?"

"As I said before, my father was an abusive man. He not only abused my mother, but he abused and molested me too. My mother was the first wife of my father. It seemed like, at times, my mother was more scared of him than I think I was. But you would never be able to tell if anything was wrong with her because she always put on this strong persona."

Brook was looking into the distance as she told her story. "Every time we went to the temple, my mother would gather with the other mothers, and they would talk about what they would cook or what pies they had made while my dad sat and talked with the other fathers. My mother would head to the kitchen every afternoon after church and put on dinner. Father would grab a bottle of whiskey and a glass and go out back cutting wood, making furniture."

Heaven scribbled on her notepad as Brook paused to wipe her nose with the Kleenex.

"At times, Mother would have me sitting in the kitchen helping her cook. One Sunday after church, my mother wasn't feeling well enough to cook, so my father made me go into the kitchen and prepare dinner.

Mother insisted she could cook dinner but just needed to lay down for a few. My father then started hollering things like, she needs to learn how to cook. Hell, pretty soon, she'll be cooking for her own husband and family. He then told my mother that if she tries to get out of bed, he'll make her regret she ever got up."

"Sounds like an asshole." Garrick's voice brought Brook back from the past.

"More like an Ike Turner to me," Heaven said.

Brook picked up her glass and drank down the vodka.

"Several months later, my mother died from cancer."

"Our condolences," Garrick muttered.

Brook's face was wet with tears, and her Kleenex had disintegrated. She reached into the box for another one.

"A few months after my mother's death, my father began to drink more heavily." He would come into my room, saying, 'you look just like your mother. It's time for you to step up and take her place. He would climb on top of me, spreading my legs, as I lay silently crying." Brook begins to sob.

"I ended up pregnant."

"My father told me if I ever told anyone he was having sex with me, he would disown me and have all the elders banish me, and I'll be looked upon as a whore."

Heaven exhaled loudly.

"After I had my baby, my father had the doula take my baby out of the room, and all I could hear in the distance was my baby crying as a horse carriage rode away."

Brook walked over to the refrigerator. "I take it you have a bottle of water in here?" she asked.

"We do! Feel free to help yourself," said Garrick.

Brook opened the refrigerator and pulled out a bottle of water. She looked at it curiously and made a face.

"Hmm, 'DRIP' water. I never heard of this brand."

"It's a black-owned water bottle company we support, located in Chicago," Heaven replied.

Brook took a sip from the bottle.

"I like the bottle's design, and I must say, it's refreshing. It has a clean, smooth crystal taste to it." She twisted the bottle cap back on the bottle.

"As you were saying," Heaven said.

"Right! As I was saying, I've never seen my baby. I do not know if I even had a boy or a girl. A few months later, I was married off to a sixty-five-year-old man named Cohyn Adams. Once married, I moved in with him and his five other wives. Since I was the youngest, they made me do most of the cleaning and sewing. The other wives put in their part too. If one was washing the dishes, the others were cooking or teaching the children in the compound school." Brook drifted off.

Heaven asked if she wanted to take a break.

"No, I'm okay. I've just never told anyone my story."

"As my partner said, if you need a break, we can pause if you like," Garrick said.

Brook placed the bottle of water on Heaven's coaster and continued.

"Once married, or should I say sold off because that's just what it felt like. I felt more like a slave. Daily chores around the clock. I was happy to go to school to be able to just sit and relax without my hands cramping up. All the girls and ladies in the house seemed to treat me differently. All except one. Emily!"

"And who was Emily?" Heaven asked.

"Emily was Cohyn's ninth wife. She was rather young, too, but older than me. Let me think." She fumbled with the bottle of water. "Emily had to be about 15. She was with child too. That's one thing I did not want to become, and that was to be with child. The night we got married, Mr. Adams took me to his room and sat me on the bed, playing with my hair. He then began to take his hands up my shirt, rubbing and squeezing my thighs. You could smell the alcohol on him. He reminded me of how my father smelled when he entered my room. His touch and stench made me want to throw up, but the next thing I know, I hear him snoring. The old man fell asleep on top of me before he could get me pregnant. I never mentioned that to him.

A few months later, I was in the yard one day hanging up the clothes I had just washed on the clothing line when Mr. Adams walked up to me. He told me there must have been something wrong with me because he planted his seed in me, and I still wasn't pregnant. He said I was useless and could see why my father gave me up. He threatened to have me inspected by the doctor and that if he found out, I couldn't bear children, I would be branded and work as a servant. If it were not for Emily putting something in his drinks the nights he came in my room to make him fall asleep, I would have been pregnant by him."

"Such a tragic story," Heaven said. "I'm sorry you had to experience those hideous things."

"If it were not for Emily, I wouldn't be sitting here talking to you now."

Brook let her mind wander back to her past, and the time she had spent as Mr. Cohyn's wife. On one particular day back then, she and Emily had been milking the cows in the barn while the other wives attended to the other chores.

"I'm going to get us out of here," Emily said, pulling out a Cell Phone from the deep pocket in her apron. "This was given to me by the nurse when I escorted one of the other wives to the doctor. The nurse works for the *Freedom Group*.

"What's the Freedom Group?"

"It's a group of women who got out of the polygamy lifestyle. They help people like us who would like to get out. They place you in a home where you could be free, wear regular clothes, and attend a regular school with regular children. Not only that...." Emily grabbed Brook's hands excitedly. "We could look at television too!"

"We could look at TV too? I can't wait! I'll pack up my clothes the night before," Brook had said.

"Shhh! Not so loud!" Emily had run to the barn doors to see if anyone were lingering around. "There is no need for you to pack up anything," She said. "You just need to be ready when it's time to go. We don't want anyone getting suspicious of what we are doing. She's been trying to get me to come for some time now, but I was scared I'd get caught. I'm with child now, and I do not want my child raised up in this type of environment."

"You're pregnant?"

"Yes"

"Mr. Adams, child?"

"Yes."

"How many months are you?"

"I haven't had my period in two months."

"How will we get away when we get to the doctor's office?"

"The driver that's escorting us will be distracted."

"Distracted! How?"

"You have no need to worry how. Just be prepared to run."

"Run! Where will I be running to?" Brook had asked, shaking her head.

"The people the nurse works for will have a truck waiting on the road. It's going to look like a utility truck. We just need to get to the truck. Once we're there, we will be free to start a new life."

In the present, Brook continued telling her story to Heaven and Garrick. Her face was no longer wet with tears, although her eyes were puffy from crying.

"That was the last time I saw Emily. We were able to get out when the nurse seemed to be having a seizure, and all eyes were on her. That's when Emily grabbed my hand, and we ran out the back of the doctor's office through the small wooded area to a dirt road. A man and woman were waiting when we reached the utility truck." She smiled softly and teared up. "Thirty years later, here I am."

"Where do we come in at?" Heaven asked.

"I would like you to help me find my child my father gave away."

Heaven and Garrick exchanged looks.

"You would like for us to find your child?" Garrick asked. "Would you happen to have a clue as to who your father may have given your baby to?"

"My father had to give my child to one of the counselors. They were always at my house conducting secret meetings."

"Do you remember the name of any of the men who met with your father in the meetings?"

"The Hierarchy would visit."

"And who is the Hierarchy?" Heaven asked.

"Yeah, I'm lost on that one," Garrick said.

"The Hierarchy is the president and two counselors of the church."

"The Hierarchy would be like the Pastor and two top deacons in the Baptist church, right? I'm asking to get a better understanding." Garrick looked at Brook, waiting on her response as he grabbed his beard.

"Garrick, I've been to African-American Baptist churches, and they are totally different from the Temple I attended. But yes, the roles are similar."

"Would you happen to know any of the men names that visited your father?" Heaven asked.

"The president was named Mr. Tibbs, and the two counselors, I do not remember their names, but I do remember one; his name was Mr. Samuel's.

He was tall and wore a patch over his left eye."

Heaven wrote this down in her notebook while Garrick got up and walked to the refrigerator.

"And what do you remember about the other two?" Heaven asked, looking up from her notebook.

"Mr. Tibbs was an older man, around sixty years old at the time. I take it he may have passed away. I don't know if Mr. Tibbs is still alive or not. And the other man, all I can remember is him being a short, plump guy around five-foot-six. And he walked with a limp. So, will you guys be able to help me?"

"With very little information, we may need more to find your child, or should I say, grown man or woman," Garrick replied.

"When I had the baby, I heard the doula say the baby had a head full of blonde hair and grey eyes. That's all I heard as she took my baby out of the room."

"I'll take it that the child took after you with the blonde hair," Garrick said.

"And as far as his eyes, my father had grey eyes too. So, will you guys be able to help me?" Brook grabbed her purse and took out her checkbook." Money will not be a problem."

"Oh, we are aware of that," Heaven said. "We just would need to know where to start." She grabbed her bottle of water and took a sip from it.

"Well, you will not be able to get onto the grounds where we stayed because of the extra security, but a big convention is coming up at the Temple, where I know people from my old compound will be in attendance."

"What type of event?" Garrick asked.

"It's called Pioneer Day."

"What type of event is that?" Heaven asked, searching 'Pioneer Day' online.

"It's a big event that ---"

Heaven cut Brook off and began reading from her computer screen, "--- It's a day commemorating the arrival of the first Mormon pioneers to Salt Lake Valley back in 1847, led by Brigham Young."

"Yes! Brigham Young. The man who took control of the Mormon church after the first founder and president John smith was murdered," Brook said. "He was considered the second president of the Mormon Church and known to have fifty-six wives."

"Damn!" Garrick said. "The man had fifty-six wives. Now that's a lot of Ass." He looked over at Brook. "Sorry, I didn't mean it like that."

So, your Mormon? No! And neither are the people who stay within that compound. The people who stay within the compound call themselves "The Submissive Angels." They are nothing like the Mormons. Just the opposite! Nothing but a knock-off extremist group.

"When is Pioneer Day?" Garrick asked.

"It's coming up in a week. This year it will be July 24th and 25th. The 24th will be the all-day religion ceremonies, and on the 25th, they will have the grand parade."

"Will this event Pioneer Day be held at the church?" Garrick asked.

"Yes, at the Temple."

Garrick looked at Heaven. "And how are we supposed to get in there? They will look at us like aliens."

Garrick and Heaven looked over at Brook.

"I suppose you'll walk in with the other people attending," Brook said.

"Not to sound funny," said Garrick, "but do you see the color of our skin? I passed that church a few times, and all I see is people of your color out there."

Brook smiled. "Oh, you may not have seen any African-Americans when you passed by the church but believe me, African American people attend. Do you know of Eldridge Cleaver?" Brook leaned back into her chair and crossed her legs.

"I see here he was one of the leaders in the Black Panther Party until he converted to the Mormon faith in 1983." Heaven was reading from her computer again.

"Trust me, you won't be alone. There are other African Americans that attend the temple too. Now, will you be able to take on this case for me?"

Heaven looked over at Garrick and then back at Brook.

"We'll take on this case for you." She started typing on her computer keyboard.

"Great! Thank you," Brook said, raising her checkbook. "How much should I write the check out for?"

"We charge Three Hundred Dollars an hour," Heaven responded. "If we need to seek extra help or resources, that will also be added to the bill."

"Money is not a problem for me," Brook said, writing in her checkbook. She ripped the check out when she finished signing it, passing it to Heaven.

Heaven's eyes widened.

Garrick stood behind Heaven to look at the check.

"From the looks on your faces, I see that check should be enough to cover your fees and anything extra you may need to help find my child."

"This will be more than enough," Heaven said surprisedly.

"One more thing I forgot to mention. The doctor's office that I and the others on the compound went to when we got sick or just for regular check-ups is still there. The doctor who was there when I visited is no longer there, but his son took over the family practice. Perhaps, you can start there."

"That's a great lead," Heaven said, "But how do you know the doctor is not there and his son took over?"

"I called one day some time ago and made like I wanted to make an appointment and asked if I could speak with Dr. Grant. To my surprise, I was transferred, and a much younger voice answered the phone. I asked to speak with an older gentleman who use to see me back then, and the younger man then told me that was his father, but he passed away and now runs the family practice."

"Good information Brook," Garrick stood up. "Excuse me, ladies?"

"Before we can start, Brook, we just need you to fill out some paperwork acknowledging that you are hiring our company to take on this case for you." Heaven reached into her desk drawer, pulled out a clipboard that held the paperwork, and passed it to Brook.

"We will also need to swab your mouth for your DNA to compare in the case we find your child."

"I'll grab one of the DNA kits," Garrick said.

"You guys just have DNA tests lying around?'

"We have clients that require DNA testing, especially for children," Heaven replied. Garrick passed the kit to Heaven.

"All I need to do is swab your mouth." Heaven stood up and walked over to the sink to wash her hands. She took out a pair of rubber gloves from the counter drawer and put them on before walking over to Brook and opening the DNA test. "That's all we need for now," she said after taking a few swabs from Brook's mouth. "We'll be in contact with you once we get more information. It's time for us to do some digging.

Chapter Two

"This check looks good. We never had anyone write us a check for this much. Do you see the zeroes on this here?" Garrick shook his head as he examined the check. "We have to cash this quickly."

"We'll do that as soon as I put something on my stomach. Heaven said as she rubbed her belly. Plus, with all the money that woman has, I don't think the check will bounce." Garrick and Heaven sat at a booth at Ruby's Diner, discussing their morning meeting with Brook.

A friendly waitress walked up to them. "Hi, my name is Gigi. Welcome to Ruby's Diner. I'll be taking care of you today. May I start you off with something to drink?"

"Can I get a glass of water for now with lemon?" Heaven asked the waitress.

"I need something stronger than water." Garrick winked at Gigi. "Let me get a coke with lite ice. Oh, and I guess I'll take some water too. Lite ice!" Garrick continued looking at the menu.

"Got it!" Two glasses of water. One with lemon and a coke. To Heaven, she asked, "Are you ready to order?"

"Please give us a few more minutes."

"No problem! I'll grab those drinks for you."

"Wait! Before you go, can you put an order of cheese sticks in for us?" Garrick asked as he continued to look at the menu.

"Sure! Which count would you like? The five or ten piece?"

"Let us get the ten-piece with extra marinara sauce."

Gigi wrote on her notepad. I'll put this in for you now. She walked away.

"So, where should we start with this mysterious case?" Garrick asked Heaven.

"Brook said the doctor's office is still there. We need to get into their records and look for the newborns he treated the year Brook's child was born thirty years ago."

"That will be around 1992, I suppose."

"I'll have Hector from Computer Forensics hack into the doctor's system to get this information for us. He'll be glad to help."

"Why, because he has a crush on you?".

"Whatever!" Heaven laughed and rolled her eyes.

A few minutes passed, and Gigi returned to the booth holding three drinks in one hand and cheese sticks in the other.

"Here are your drinks and cheese sticks. Are you about ready to order?"

"I believe we are," Garrick said, smiling at Gigi. "I'll take your turkey burger with cheese, lettuce, tomatoes, pickles, onions, and mayo. No ketchup!"

"Will you like fries with that or another side?"

"I'll take the homemade fries with a side of BBQ sauce."

"You'll eat BBQ sauce but won't eat ketchup. Hmm, weird!" Heaven said.

"And for you, ma'am?" Gigi asked, turning to Heaven.

"I'll take the chicken cob salad with extra blue cheese crumbles and bacon. Thank you! That will be it for me."

"Sounds great! I'll put this right in for you guys." Gigi walked back to the kitchen.

"Like I was saying, I'll reach out to Hector. In the meantime, you go do what you do best."

"And what's that?" Garrick asked as he sipped on the coke.

"Be nosy!" Heaven laughed as she dipped a cheese stick into the marinara sauce.

"Nosy gets the cases solved."

"Can't argue with you on that. Anyways, go snoop around the old compound Brook stayed on and see what you can find," Heaven said.

"Now, how in the hell am I to get into that compound when Brook said it's sewed up like Fort Knox?"

Heaven smirked. Hmm, "I'm quite sure you're familiar with how to get into tight things."

"You should know!" Garrick clapped back. "But, I guess I can go take a look around the compound and get my Inspector Gadget on."

Hector was sitting at his desk in his office, eyes glued to his computer screens when Heaven walked in.

"I see you're still at it," she said to him.

He spun his chair around to face Heaven. She was struck by how handsome he was. He stood at 6ft 5in, with long curly black hair and military tattoos.

"Ah, Detective Campbell! I meant 'Private Investigator Campbell'", what brings you this way?"

"I need you to do me a little favor."

"Sure thing! As long as it does not involve the IRS or NASA." He chuckled softly.

"Garrick and I are working on a case, and I need you to hack into this doctor's office system and get me the names of newborns he treated back in 1992."

"Hmm, 1992! The same year them four officers were acquitted of beating Rodney King."

"I see you know your cases," Heaven said, looking surprised.

Hector spun his chair back around to look at his computer screen. "What's the name of the doctor's office?"

"It's called Grant Family Practice, and it's located right here in LA."

Hector turned to his computer, opening up one of his hacking programs, and typed in the name of the doctor's office.

"I'm locked on," he said.

Heaven sighed. "I knew you were the right person to help me with this. I see you've gotten faster and better now." She touched Hector's shoulder gently and smiled, bending over to look at his computer screen.

"1992, right?" he asked, wiping a dab of sweat from his forehead.

"Yes! Can you please pull up all the records of the newborns treated there that year and the names of their parents?"

"Give me a few hours, and I will have all you need."

Heaven straightened up as Hector spun around in the chair to face her. She eyed the apparent bulge in Hector's pants. He noticed this and smiled.

"I'm not here just on business. I'm happy to see you as well, Hector."

"Yeah!" Hector responded.

Heaven walked to the door, and Hector followed her. When she reached the door, she locked it.

"Before I leave, though – "she turned around and placed her hand on Hector's bulge – "we also have some personal business to take care of." She started gently rubbing Hector's manhood through his jeans.

Hector sighed. "So, I see you want something else too."

Yeah! And what is that? Heaven said in a low, whispering

voice.

Hector grabbed Heaven and pushed her back to the wall. Heaven pushed back with her hips, unbuckled Hector's belt, and unzipped them to expose his rock-hard dick. Before his pants and belt dropped to the floor, he pulled a condom out of his wallet.

"Let me see what that bulge is all about," Heaven said, lifting her skirt and turning around to place her hands on the wall. Hector slowly pushed his hard dick into her, and she moaned. Her wet pussy gripped his dick, and they both began to climax almost immediately.

Hector rested against the wall, his erect dick hanging out of his pants. He was drained of all energy. Heaven started fixing herself up. "I see you enjoyed this kitten," she said.

"Hmm, more like the lion's den, he responded in a heavy voice."

Heaven pulled out her compact mirror from her purse and brushed her hair back into place. "I hope to hear from you soon regarding what you find."

Hector pulled up his pants, zipping them up.

"You can have this dick anytime," he mumbled.

"Excuse me! I didn't hear you."

"I said you'll have that info. Give me a few hours."

"Great! Oh, and Hector, this stays between us. No kissing and telling, or you won't be entering this lion's den anymore," she said as she left.

Garrick's car was parked a distance from the compound. His binoculars zoomed in on the property. A woman's face came into view, and he zoomed in closer to see who she was.

"What the hell is Detective Pratt doing here, and why is she dressed like that?" he muttered. Pushing a button on the binoculars, he took snapshots and videos.

"Wait until I tell Heaven about this."

Heaven walked into her master bedroom and sat on the chaise lounge, taking her clothes off. She then walked into the bathroom wearing only her panties. She turned on the water in her ALFI brand 65' inch soaking bathtub and poured bubble bath into the water. The scent of vanilla filled the air. She returned to her room, pulled out her phone, and connected it to the charger.

"Alexa, play Usher," she said to the room.

Alexa's voice floated through the house. "Getting Usher from Heaven's music library." Usher's climax began to play softly, and Heaven's phone rang.

"Call from Sister!" Alexa announced. "Answer or ignore?"

"She would call when I'm trying to relax," Heaven muttered. "Answer!" She picked up her earpiece and placed it in her right ear, then grabbed her robe off the back door of her closet and put it on.

"Sis! What took you so long to answer?" Nevaeh asked.

"Damn girl, can you chew that gum any louder? And your butt better be glad I answered the phone anyways. I'm about to eat, then relax in my new bathtub with some Mary J. Blige wine, of course."

Heaven heard Nevaeh chuckle on the other end of the phone. "You always doing old lady shit. That's why you need a man."

"Trust m! I don't need a man. If I want some ass, I know how to get it with no strings attached."

Heaven walked to the bathroom and turned the water off. "Anyways, Nevaeh, what's going on?" She walked to the kitchen and started pulling out some leftover shrimp fried rice and a chicken eggroll from the refrigerator.

"Girl, nothing! Just calling to see what's up with you."

"And to talk about Devonte?"

"Girl, Devonte is not on my mind. As a matter of fact, I'm about to go have drinks with a friend."

"Yeah, a friend. So, who is this friend, and where you meet this friend at?"

"I met her at one of Drelow's parties."

Heaven stared at her phone, shocked.

"You're going to have drinks with a woman you met at Drelows?" She opened the microwave and took out her food. Then she went to the wine cooler sitting on the marble counter, and grabbed a bottle of Bartenura Moscato sweet.

"Yeah! She's a personal trainer, and I thought it would be good to have her train me. I told you I was doing that marathon to support Alopecia."

"I'll have to admit, running those marathons is not a joke," Heaven said as she poured herself some wine. "You have to be fit to do something like that." She took a sip of the wine and pulled out a fork from her dish rack.

"Plus, she has a lot of clients I would like to get into the salon," Nevaeh said.

"I hear you puffing over there."

"Yeah, Drelow hooked me up with some gas. This Snoop OG shit smoking hard. Hell, I need to get my appetite up."

Heaven laughed at her twin. "Your butt likes to eat! So, where are you all meeting up at? Oh, and how old is this trainer?"

"She's around our age, and we're meeting at some place downtown. She says it's a new black-owned winery that serves food and has a live band."

"Ok, that sounds nice. Have fun and be safe, Nevaeh. Oh, and please don't drive this girl cray cray like you did the girl in college. What's her name again?"

"Her name was Casey, and I did not drive her cray cray! She just had separation issues."

"Separation issues, my ass. You had the girl jumping out of trees and shit. Doing drive-by pull-ups."

"Anyways, I can't help if she was pussy whipped."

"Girl, like I said, have fun, be safe, and I'm about to hang up so I can go relax in my new tub."

"I forgot you bought an ALFI," Nevaeh said, "I'm going to have to come over and try that out."

"Goodnight, Nevaeh!"

"I'm for real. I can see my body soaking in it now."

"Goodnight, Nevaeh!" Heaven said with finality, hanging up the phone. She finished the last bite of rice, placed the plate into the dishwasher, and turned it on.

Heaven walked into her room with the wine glass and bottle in hand. She placed them on her dresser, took off her robe, and then her panties.

"Alexa, play TEMS."

"Getting Tems from Heaven's playlist," Alexa said.

Tems' "Crazy Things" came on, and Heaven moved her body to the music as she entered her bathroom with the wine bottle and glass.

She slid into the water and picked up the washcloth that was hanging by the side of the bathtub. She dipped the cloth into the warm water, wrung it out, and wiped her face.

Her phone rang again. This time, it was Hector calling. She reached for her phone on the fluffy pink bath rug next to the tub and answered it.

"Hey, Hector! I was waiting for you to call. I hope you have some good news for me." She slid back down in the tub, her phone in one hand and the wine glass in the other.

"Like I said, before you left my office, I'll find what I can for you, and to my surprise, I found out that there were a few newborns born in 1992 that Davis Senior had as patients from the compound you mentioned. Two were fraternal twins named Julia and Jacob. Their parents are Scott and Jill Lancing. A girl named Susan was born to a Brandon and Mildred Samuels'. The last was a boy, born to Ammon and Elizabeth Moore."

Heaven sat up in the tub.

"I haven't even got to the good part yet," Hector continued. "Something told me to dig deeper into the mother's medical records. So, me being me, that's what I did. Mrs. Elizabeth Moore, maiden name Elizabeth Ryan, had emergency surgery when she was 16 years old."

"Surgery for what?" Heaven asked.

"She had a miscarriage. Her records also noted that they had to take her uterus due to cervical cancer."

"So, how did she pull that off being pregnant if she couldn't have children?"

"You're the Private Investigator, and that's your job to find out. Now, I did my part. Can I see you again?"

"Perhaps," Heaven said, sipping her wine slowly.

"It's like that?"

"Like I said, I'll think about it. Thanks for the info. I'll call you if I need more."

"More info or more of me?"

"I'll talk to you later, Hector. Bye!"

At their office, Garrick was sitting at his chair, with his feet cocked up on his desk, eating a bowl of "Proud Puff" cereal when Heaven walked in.

"Good morning Garrick!"

"Morning, Ms. Campbell! I made some fresh coffee and bought some donuts." He took his feet off the desk and wiped the milk off his mouth with the tip of his necktie.

"I see you're eating my cereal too, Mr.I-don't-do-gluten-free," Heaven chuckled.

"This cereal gluten-free?" Garrick stood up and walked over to the fridge. He grabbed the cereal box off the top of the refrigerator and examined it. "Damn, your right. It is gluten-free."

"And it's also the first black cereal out on the market. The guy that started the company name is Nic King, and the company is called "Legacy Cereal" based out of New York."

"That's what's up! Hell, they're making black superheroes. Why not have a black cereal brand? I'll admit, It's good."

Heaven walked over to her desk and placed her leather tote bag on it. Then she went to the coffee machine.

"Was Hector able to give you anything?"

Heaven poured herself some coffee. "Yeah, he gave me some, alright," she said, smiling to herself and grabbing two packs of sugar.

"So, what did he say?"

"There were a few children born Davis Senior took care of in 1992 from that compound."

"I'll admit, Hector stepped his game up," Garrick said, sounding impressed.

Heaven's mind drifted off to Hector's office, him pounding into her against the wall.

"Hmm, what got you smiling over there from cheek to cheek? Will it be the reason why you didn't answer your phone last night," Garrick said.

"Boy, I'm smiling cheek to cheek because I finally got me some rest. And I didn't answer my phone because I was in the tub relaxing. Trying to enjoy some me time." Heaven sipped her coffee. "So, did you find anything at the compound?"

"Brook was right! That place is locked down like Fort Knox. There are two big gates at the compound entrance that are guarded. I mean, they have walls and barb wire on them too. Oh, and them boys packing them big guns. Some military shit."

Heaven sat back in her chair and pulled her cell phone out of her bag.

"I was able to climb a tree to take a look over the gates. The compound is full of homes, and the grounds are guarded too. They looked like they were having a town hall meeting or gathering. You wouldn't believe this, though. I saw Detective Pratt."

"Detective Pratt from the precinct?" Heaven sat up in her chair. "What the hell was she doing there?"

"I said the same thing."

"Well, we're about to find out," Heaven said, grabbing her bag. "Time to go talk to Detective Pratt."

Chapter Three

"Girl, now hook me up. I have a date tonight." Drelow, an eccentric trans-woman in her forties, was sitting in Nevaeh's salon chair.

"Who you got a date with?" Nevaeh asked her as she turned on the blow dryer.

"Girl, you know you're nosy, but since you asked." Drelow pulled up a picture of a man dressed in doctor scrubs. "This is my date for tonight."

"Girl, he's fine! Where in the hell did you meet him at?"

"He attended one of my parties. He began talking to me at the bar, and I told him I was the party's host. He then started to tell me how nice everything was and how he was looking to have a nice time and get away from the operating room."

"So, girl, he's a surgeon?"

"Girl, a heart surgeon at that. Enough about me, what happened with you and the trainer?"

"Let's just say after we left the bar, my pussy was her dessert."

"Girl, I knew you were going to let her smash that ass."

"On the for real, for real, she did the damn thing. I haven't had my pussy eaten like that in a long time."

"I heard she's good with that long tongue."

"YEAH, the tongue is good! But, then I told her she had to bounce."

"Just like a Nigga, you straight treated her after you got some head."

"Nah, it wasn't like that. I just didn't want her to think we have something going on since I gave her some of my cookie."

Someone walked into the shop.

"Girl, who is this thick, fine, ass man walking up in here?" Drelow asked as he sized the man up as he walked towards them.

"What the fuck is he doing here?" Nevaeh said as she frowned.

"You know him?"

"Girl, that's my cheating ex-husband Devonte."

"Oh, Mr. Football Star? I thought he was in Atlanta."

"His cheating ass was traded here to L.A."

Devonte approached them, looking sexy in a Giorgio Armani three-piece royal blue suit with a collarless white shirt. He was holding a dozen red roses.

"Hi, Nevaeh!" he said.

"Devonte, what the hell are you doing here?"

"I know roses are your favorite, so I decided to stop by and surprise you."

Drelow took in Devonte's Jean-Paul Cologne as she fanned herself with a Chinese designer hand fan. "Nice big shoes there!" she said.

Devonte looked down at his shoes.

"Devonte, why are you here?"

"I thought I'll surprise you and drop by since I'll be playing in LA now."

"I think walking in on a bitch sucking your dick was surprising enough. I don't need or want this surprise or your roses."

Drelow rolled her eyes at Devonte and began to fan herself faster.

"Look, Nevaeh, I'll admit, I fucked up, but that was over a year ago. I miss you." He tried to give Nevaeh the roses.

"So, you coming up in here with roses is supposed to do what?" Nevaeh grabbed the roses and tossed them into the trash can next to her booth. "I don't want anything from your cheating ass."

"I'm human, Nevaeh, and I wasn't thinking at the time. I haven't been the same since our divorce."

"And! I don't give a fuck."

"Look, let me make it up to you. Snoop Dogg is throwing a charity football event that he's invited me to, and I know there will be many women there who would love to know more about your shop."

Nevaeh continued styling Drelow's hair. "Hmm, you say Snoop Dogg?"

"Yup, Snoop, and other celebrities."

"I heard about Snoop throwing this event to raise money to get uniforms to all the grammar schools and high schools in Compton. He do throw great parties. The last charity event he threw was on a 100-foot yacht, and it was one of the best parties I ever went to in my life," Drelow said frantically. "Girl, fuck that stubborn shit. You better go, or I'll go for you," she whispered to Nevaeh.

"You expect me to say yes, like ain't shit happened between us? Like we're not fucking divorced?"

Devonte put his hands shyly in his pockets. "I'm here to say I am truly sorry, and I do apologize for fucking our marriage up. I was wrong, baby, and I apologize from the bottom of my heart."

"Girl, Let the man finish talking and see what he has to offer before you go opening up your ratchet mouth," Drelow said.

"I don't care what he has to offer."

Devonte pulled out a red box wrapped with a black silk bow from his pants pocket.

"I truly do apologize, baby. I do!" He said.

"Girl, stop being a bitch and take the box," Drelow looked at Nevaeh, twisting her lips.

Nevaeh took the box from Devonte.

"Again, I am sorry. I know this may not make up for the pain I caused, but I hope you understand that I am sorry and truly miss you. I miss us!"

"Girl, open the damn box."

Nevaeh opened the box while Drelow and Devonte watched.

"A key, Devonte!"

"Not just any key."

Devonte grabbed Nevaeh's hand and pressed the alarm button on the key.

Everyone looked towards the shop's front window as they walked towards the front door.

"Girl, tell me that's not a Ferrari," Drelow said in a surprised tone.

Devonte said, "Hmm, I see you know your cars. As a matter of fact, It's an 812 GTS Ferrari convertible with a 789-horsepower engine with a seven-speed transmission."

"Shut up!" Drelow said, trying to grab the keys out of Nevaeh's hand.

They all went outside—Nevaeh with a stunned look on her face.

"Devonte, you bought me a car and a Ferrari convertible at that. I don't know what to say. This is beautiful." She walked around the car, taking a closer look at it while Drelow took a selfie with the car. Devonte went up to Nevaeh and tilted her chin so that he was looking into her eyes.

"I'm not saying forgiveness will happen overnight, but it's been over a year, and I'm asking you to please forgive me. I'll do whatever it takes to get my wife back."

"Girl, if you don't take him back, another hoochie will," Drelow said softly under her breath.

Nevaeh looked at her and Devonte's reflection in the car's tinted window. "Devonte, I would love to accompany you to the charity event, but I can't promise you that we'll get back together. That will take some time." I need to be able to trust you again.

"Take all the time you need, baby. I'm just asking that you think about it."

"I'll think about it."

Devonte hugged her gently and kissed her on the cheek.

"Here is my new address and number. Just in case you would like to come check out my new place. Plus, I can use a hand with decorating, and you could bring your friend with you too."

Drelow, who had gone live on social media, continued posing and taking pictures of the car. Devonte opened the car door taken out a basket. He then passed it to Nevaeh.

"I see you left the car on," she said.

"Yeah, for the basket."

"So, what's in the basket?"

Drelow said excitedly, "Looks like more gifts, Nevaeh! Honey, that cat must been good."

"Bitch! It's still good." She looked at Devonte and then pulled back the blanket to reveal an all-brown, curly-haired Havanese puppy with a white strip of hair on its chest and neck.

"Oh my God, Devonte, you bought me a puppy and a Havanese at that."

"I remember the stories you used to tell me about the Havanese dog you and your sister had as children until it was stolen."

"You remember that?" Nevaeh kissed Devonte on the cheek as she pulled the dog out of the basket and placed it on her chest. Drelow filmed them with her phone.

Awe, now this some real cute shit here Drelow said as she continued to record.

"I remember a lot, baby. Just give us one day at a time, and I promise I will make it up to you."

"Girl, we're human! We fuck up. Give this fine ass man another chance, or I'll take him," Drelow said.

"Hey, your name is Drelow, right? I respect you for being yourself, and I heard about you having dope ass parties too, but I'm strictly a surfboard man, but I will tell you, I have a cousin that's into what you're into." Maybe I can introduce you to him someday.

"If he's fine as your ass, I'll...."

"Girl, stop!" Nevaeh cut Drelow off. "And yes, his cousin Big Tone is fine but in Atlanta."

"Bitch, it's planes," Drelow said.

Devonte watched Naveah as she admired the puppy. "I'm glad you like your gifts. Don't forget to grab yourself something nice to wear for the charity event this weekend." He reached into his wallet, pulled out a Black American Express Centurion Card, and passed it to her. "Get whatever you want. I have to go do a press conference. I'll see you this weekend." he said, walking back to his range rover.

"Bitchhhhhh!" Drelow said when Devonte had driven off, "You got the man wanting you back. If I were you, I'd give him another chance."

"That's just it, you're not me, and I don't know if I should give him another chance after walking in on him and a bitch in our bed. In our house, at that."

Nevaeh leaned back on the car and held the puppy to her chest.

"Girl, I know it ain't been long since we've known each other but bitch, you ain't no damn angel. You act like you have never fucked up before or never hurt anybody's feelings. I remember you telling me about that fling you had with that woman in college and how you were fucking around on her with a guy, so you were not being honest with her or yourself but up here trying to throw rocks."

Drelow took the puppy from Nevaeh and started petting it.

"Now, if you don't want him, I'm sure there are women lined up, ready to snatch him up. Hell, the man bought you an expensive-ass car and a cute-ass puppy. At least give him a chance, and if it doesn't work out, you can always have the trainer tame that ass. But regardless of what you decide bitch, this car and dog stays. *Facts, Baby, Facts*!" Drelow said as they both started laughing.

"Now, lock this damn shop up, and let's take this baby on the expressway and blow it out."

Chapter Four

The dimly lit police bar was rowdy with activity when Heaven and Garrick walked in. A retirement party was in full swing. Heaven and Garrick walked over to the bar and greeted some fellow officers there as the bartender approached them.

"Look what the devil dragged in. If it ain't our two famous Private Investigators," said the Bartender.

"What up, Stanley! Let me get a Honey Hennessey on the rocks."

"And I'll have a glass of Libby Pink Moscato," Heaven said.

The bartender started making their drinks.

"Who's retiring?" Garrick asked.

"Lieutenant Williams!"

"Well, I guess it's about that time. He's been on the force for over thirty years. Hell, I thought after his wife went to jail for the murder of the mayor's daughter, he'd retire then."

Just then, the rowdy crowd started chanting noisily, demanding a speech. Lieutenant Williams took command of the room.

"I would like to say thank you guys for coming and seeing my old ass off."

The crowd laughed.

"It was nice working with you guys, and I must admit, I won't miss none of you."

The crowd laughed again.

"Now, drink, and eat up. The tap is on you, taxpayers."

Lieutenant Williams giggled as he took a sip of his beer and walked over to the bar where heaven and Garrick sat.

"Garrick, Heaven, it's been a minute."

"Congratulations on your retirement," Heaven said.

"What are your plans now that you'll be leaving the precinct?" Garrick asked.

"Chemo! In Florida."

Heaven's eyes widened. "Chemo! You have cancer, Lieu?"

"No, not me! It's my wife, and it's breast cancer. No one knows, so please keep this between us."

"Stanley, let me get another Miller," The lieutenant gestured to the bartender before turning to Garrick. "She's locked up in the Women's Reception Center but is receiving treatment at one of the cancer hospitals in Florida. Regardless of what she did, she's still my wife and needs me now. I take the blame for what happened. I should never had an affair on my wife. She wouldn't be locked up if it wasn't for me."

The lieutenant grabbed the cold bottle of beer and walked back towards the crowd.

Heaven and Garrick watched the Lieutenant disappear into the sea of dark blue and white shirts in the bar.

"Damn! First, his wife is convicted of murder for killing the mayor's daughter because of her affair with the Lieu. She also tried to put a bullet in the Lieutenant's head. Now she has breast cancer."

"He's a stronger man than I thought. I mean, she tried to put a bullet in the man's head right in front of us," Heaven said.

Garrick gestured to the bartender to pour him another drink. "If you didn't shoot her, hell, maybe we'll all be dead."

"Bingo! There's Detective Pratt." Heaven looked, swallowing her drink and following Pratt, who was walking towards the ladies' room. Garrick grabbed his drink, too, and moved in the direction of the two ladies.

Inside the ladies' room, Garrick and Heaven waited by the sink for Pratt to come out of the bathroom stall. She was surprised when she saw them. "Heaven and Garrick! What are you doing in here?"

"I'm a lady, so I believe I'm in the right place," Heaven said. Pratt moved to the sink and started washing her hands.

"We need to talk to you," Garrick said. Heaven looked into the other bathroom stalls to ensure they were all alone.

"Look, we're working a case, and when looking into a location involving the case we're working, Garrick noticed you were there."

"I was where?"

"At the compound," Garrick answered.

"The compound outside of LA. *You know, the Submissive Angels.* Can you tell us what you were doing there?" Heaven looked at Pratt with a curious look on her face.

"It's confidential!"

"Detective Pratt, perhaps, we can work together on this," Heaven suggested.

Pratt looked around the bathroom. "We can't talk here. Garrick, I believe you still have my number. Call me, and we can talk later. Too many eyes in here watching." She opened the bathroom door and walked away.

"You got her number, huh? You need to be using that number ASAP and do whatever you must to do to get as much information out of her," Heaven reacted. She washed her hands, drying them with paper towels and tossing them into the trash can.

"I don't care if you have to use your Mandingo as you did before," she giggled.

They walked back to the bar, and Heaven gestured for the bartender to get her another drink.

"Pink Moscato coming up." The bartender said, placing a chilled wine glass in front of Heaven pouring her a Pink Moscato. Heaven picked up her drink. "Like Pratt said, you got her number, so use it to find out why the hell she was there and what's going on."

Garrick downed his second shot of Hennessey and chuckled.

"So, now you're pimping me out?"

Naveah sat on her couch, legs crossed in yoga position. She lit up a blackwood full of Snoop Dog weed and took a long leisurely drag from it. Then she dialed a number on her phone.

"Hey, Sis! I haven't heard from you in a few days. I call, and your phone goes straight to voicemail."

Heaven's voice came through the line. "I just been busy working on a case for a client. What's going on? Everything ok?"

"Look, I have something to tell you, and I don't need to hear all the judgmental shit either. I called to talk to you as my sister, not the Private Investigator."

"What happened now?"

"Let's just say I have a new Havanese puppy, and it's just like the one we use to have as kids before it was stolen."

"You didn't tell me you were going to get a dog and an expensive one at that.

"I didn't! It was a gift.

"From who? The trainer?"

"You should see him, Heaven. I'm sending pictures to your phone now, and I'm also sending you another picture of my other baby."

When Heaven saw the pictures, she said, "Wait is this a Ferrari?"

"Yes, sis! My new toy."

"How the hell did you get a Ferrari? Who fucking hair are you doing to be able to afford a damn Ferrari? Did Drelow hook you up? Damn, is the trainer getting money like that?"

"I wish! Devonte bought me the car and the puppy."

A disappointed look crossed Heaven's face.

"Sis, Devonte came up to my shop while I was doing Drelow hair and pulled out a box. I opened the box, and it was a key. I get outside, and there sits a Ferrari, black and red with tented windows. Devonte opens the door and pulls out a basket covered with a white cloth."

Heaven shook her head as she listened.

"In the basket was the puppy."

"Devonte comes up to your shop and gives you an expensive ass car and puppy. I take it you jumped on his dick after that."

"No, I jumped on his dick after he took me to the Snoop Dog Charity event."

"You were there?"

"Yes! And I networked with many celebrities who will be coming to my shop now to get their hair and nails done after seeing what I was working with. Girl, I was sharp as hell. Hair and nails were on point."

"Hmm, so, do this mean you're taking him back?"

"Sis, you know me better than that. I got him thinking it's all good. I can't trust him like that, but he can give me all the gifts and clients I need. He's bagging, so I'll let him bag and play his ass like he did me."

"Be careful! A man likes to play the game, but they do not like when the game is played on them."

"I hear you, Heaven, but it's my time. I'll talk with you later. My bell is ringing."

"Who at your door? Devonte?"

"Let's just say it's time for some physical therapy, and the trainer is in the house."

"Wow! Good night, Nevaeh."

Chapter Five

Garrick pulled up into the driveway, where Detective Pratt sat on the porch awaiting. He stepped out of his BMW 4 series with two dozen roses, looking like Tubbs from Miami Vice, in an all-cream linen suit, with a muscle shirt and Gucci loafers.

"Well, damn! I see being a Private Investigator is paying off." Pratt said to him.

"I can't complain."

"Thank you for the roses. I see you still know what I like."

Garrick smiled at her. "You called and said you have some information for me."

Pratt put the roses up to her nose and smelled them.

"Yes! I do."

Inside her house, she put the roses in a vase.

"I'm out of Hennessey, but I have Vodka and Tequila."

"Vodka will be great."

"On the rocks?"

"I see you still know how I like it." Garrick smiled! Exposing his pretty white teeth.

She poured Garrick a double shot of Vodka and herself a shot of

Tequila. She passed Garrick the drink and sat down beside him. "Let's

get right to it."

Garrick sat up, drink in hand. "Look, I was at the compound looking into a lead for a case we're working on. Then, I see you there in what looks to be a town meeting. Why were you there, Pratt?"

"The same reason you were there. On a case."

"What case?"

"You know I'm not inclined to tell you that."

"Come on! You're talking to me, Pratt."

He grabbed her knee and rubbed it gently.

Pratt downed her Tequila, stood up, and moved to the bar to pour herself another shot. "You know I haven't seen you in a while, and now you're over here rubbing on my knee."

"No, it's not like that. You've been busy, and I started a new business, and we have not been able to have time like we use to. Plus, you're married, remember!"

"As you can see, that's over."

"Oh, I didn't know."

"Yeah, as you said, you've been busy. I was shocked to find out that Lieutenant William's wife was the one that killed the mayor's daughter." Pratt said as she sipped the drink.

"Yeah, I didn't believe it, but she confessed after Heaven shot her."

"Yeah, I heard about that. Glad to see you guys made it out of that situation ok. Would you like another drink?"

"Sure!"

Garrick brushed up against Pratt as she poured him the drink. This made her body tingle, and she quickly sat back down on the couch. "We have evidence that a polygamy turned prostitution ring is being run out of that compound, and the girls are being drugged."

"Who's your source?"

Pratt took another sip of her drink. "Me! I used to be one of those girls."

Garrick sat down next to Pratt. He was looking at her tenderly.

"I was coming home from school one day, and a black van pulled up as I was tying my shoe. Two men jumped out, grabbed me, tossing me into a van. They placed a rag over my nose, and the next thing you know, I woke up in a small room with a mattress that smelled of urine and feces and a red bucket for me to shit and pee in."

Garrick's eyebrows shot up.

"After a year of being doped up, I was finally able to get out."

Garrick wrapped his arms around Pratt's shoulders.

"I remember it like yesterday. I remember the night I was finally able to get away. I was taken to one of the bidders' locations, and drinks were waiting. The trick tried to give me a roofie like they all do to have complete control of your body. I told him I did not want a drink, but he insisted and passed it to me. He then went into the bathroom, and that's when I switched the drinks. After a few minutes, he began acting drowsy and passed out. I ran out of the room and out the back door. I kept running, following the train tracks that led into the city. That's when I met a woman named Emily, who was on the street passing out flyers for young women looking for shelter who had nowhere to go. She took me in, where I met other young women like myself. That's what made me want to become a cop, to put mutherfuckers like them under the jail."

"Wow, I never would have known. Did you say the lady who took you in name was Emily?"

"Yes! If it weren't for her and her daughter helping me, I wouldn't be here today. I haven't seen her in a while. She married a Baptist pastor, and they moved to Louisiana."

"My client mentioned a Emily. She hired us to find her child that she gave birth to when she was 13 years old, but she do not know if the child she gave birth to was a girl or a boy. That's why we are investigating the compound to find this mysterious child. I see it's like Fort Knox getting up in there. How were you able to get in without them knowing who you are?" Garrick said with a puzzled look on his face.

"I've been around them long enough to know how they think, so getting in wasn't hard. Plus, my body and looks have changed since then, so they have no clue who the hell I am. Especially with the wig and a little bodywork. I also have an agent on the inside working with me."

"An Agent! You're working with the Feds?"

"There you go again, asking a lot of questions." Pratt paused for a minute. "The person you're looking for, do you have a name?"

"No, we were told he has blond hair and crystal grey eyes. He should be in his late 20's or early 30's."

Pratt sat back on the couch, thinking. "Blond hair! Gray eyes! Hmm, that sounds like counselor Moore's son."

"Counselor Moore!"

"Yeah, Old Man Moore. He's one of the counselors at the church.

"How old is this, Mr. Moore?"

"The father looks to be in his late 60's early 70's. The son looks to be in his late 20's or early 30's."

Garrick stood up with the empty rock glass in his hand. "This could be the same person my client hired us to look for." He walked back over to the bar and poured himself more Vodka.

"Hmm! How does his old man look? Mr. Moore! What color is the old man hair and eyes?"

"His father is a short man that stands around my height and walks with a limp. He has salt and pepper hair, and it's thin. If I'm not mistaken, he has blue eyes."

"And you say the father walks with a limp? And what about his mother? How do she look?"

"Now, you got me feeling like I'm being interrogated, Mr. Garrick!"

"I'm just trying to put pieces of the puzzle together."

"Well, his mother is a small-framed woman."

"What color is her hair?"

"Burnette, with some greyish-white streaks."

"So, your sure the blond head guy has gray eyes?"

"His name is Clay. Clay Moore! And yes, he has crystal gray eyes."

"And what's his old man name?"

"His father's name is Ammon, and his mother's name is Elizabeth."

"This ring your trying to bring down, who are the key players."

"His name is Mr. Samuel's. He has his goons go out and look for girls who are randoms or are on drugs or runaways. Strays, as they say. He gives them drugs, food, and clothes and pimps them out. Some of the girls will do anything for him; when I say anything, I mean anything. Some think he's like a father to them. They will lie for him, steal for him, and do whatever he asks them. We just need to prove it all."

"Hmm, a low-key Don Juan."

"Pioneer Day is coming up, and there will be all types of festivities going on at the compound, so it will be busy. We'll invite you and Heaven in as our guests. I'll let Agent Charles in on this. Once we're all on the compound, we may find what we're all looking for."

"I promise, we're going to get Mr. Don Juan and his whole damn crew," Garrick said, kissing Pratt softly on the lips, then pulling back.

"I'm sorry, I should go." He started walking towards the front door, but Pratt stopped him.

"Don't go!" She stood up and walked over to him. When she reached him, she kissed him softly on the lips.

"You sure about this?" he asked.

She led Garrick up the stairs. "Do you not miss this?"

Garrick saw that she was looking at him lustfully.

"Yes, I do!"

"Well, come show me."

The following day at their office, Garrick told Heaven everything he had learned from Pratt the night before, not leaving out the details of what had happened when Pratt led him to her bedroom.

"Ok! I don't need to hear about you and Pratt passing body fluids," Heaven said, slamming down her mug on the desk.

"Do I detect some jealousy?"

"Hell Nah, you don't! Now, back to the case. A prostitution ring? You're telling me they're running a prostitution ring out of that compound?"

Garrick got up and went to the refrigerator. He opened it and grabbed a bottle of orange juice.

"What else she say?" Heaven asked.

"She says it's a man named Clay Moore who fits the description Brook gave us of her child. Remember, Brook said men came to her house to visit her father. She said one of the guys walked with a limp, but she didn't know his name."

"Yeah!" heaven responded, gripping her coffee cup.

"Pratt said the guy's name is Ammon Moore, and his wife's name is Elizabeth Moore."

"You got more info than I expected you to." I guess you slanged that dick good.

"You should know." Garrick chuckled!

"Pioneer Day is coming up in a few days, and Pratt said we can get into the compound with her as visitors from out of town."

Heaven picked up her phone and dialed it. "Hi Brook, this is Heaven. We have a lead on your case, and we will be looking into this lead in a few days. We believe you have a son, Brook."

"I have a son? How do you know this? How do you know it's my child?"

"We have someone on the inside of the compound who says they may know who your son is. We will be going into the compound as visitors for the festivities. I'll call you as soon as I know more."

"Oh my God, thank you, Heaven!"

Garrick walked back to his desk and sat down as Heaven hung up.

"This shit is deeper than we thought. This reminds me of the Oprah

Winfrey show when she investigated polygamy in Eldorado, Texas, on the yearning for Zion ranch. How the hell are we going to pull this off? We're going to need to get some costume gear to fit in."

Garrick stood up and went over to the long dress mirror that hung on one of the office walls. He struck a pose and stared thoughtfully at his reflection.

"And I know just who to call to hook us up. Drelow!" Heaven said, shaking her head like *YEAH*. She picked up her cell phone.

Drelow was in the fabric station of her mansion when her phone rang. "Hey, what's up good twin!"

"Hey, Drelow! Garrick and I are working a case for a client, and we need you to hook us up on some costumes we can wear to pull this off."

"You know I got you. What you need?"

"We need to dress like we're Mormons."

"Girl, so you and Garrick need to look like Fred and Serena."

"Who the hell is Fred and Serena?"

"Girl, you never seen The Handmaid's Tale? They dress just like the Mormons and the Amish. Hell, they seem to be the same to me. When do you need the costumes?"

"We'll need them as soon as possible."

"Glad I have a ballroom full of costumes. I already have your size, and from the look of Garrick, I sized him up already."

"I bet you have." Heaven giggles!

"Anyways, let me dig into my closet of costumes to see what I can pull out. I'll put something together for you too. I will be seeing your sister later.

Would you like me to give her the costumes, or would you like to drive up to my mansion to pick them up?"

"You can give them to Nevaeh. She gave me a spare key and been begging me to come over. I'll grab them from her house, and Drelow, do not tell her I'm coming over. I want it to be a surprise."

Girl, I got you! She'll be happy to see you. Holla! Drelow hung up the phone.

Chapter Six

When Heaven pulled up at Nevaeh's House at night, she saw Nevaeh's car in the garage and two other vehicles parked in the driveway. One was A 2022 dark blue Mercedes-Benz G63 truck, and the other was a candy apple red 2022 Jaguar F- PACE SVR. Heaven could hear loud music from inside as she walked up to the door. She rang the bell twice, but no one answered, so she pulled her keys out of her purse and opened the door with the spare key Nevaeh gave her.

As she pushed open the door, she was hit by the strong scent of marijuana.

"Nevaeh? Nevaeh!" she called out. There was no answer.

"Now, I know she is here," Heaven muttered. "Her car and two other cars are in the driveway. Can't nobody hear shit with this loud ass music playing."

She scanned the house as she walked into the kitchen and opened the refrigerator to grab a bottle of water. Then, she followed the sound of the music up the stairs. As she got closer to the bedroom, she could see a red light and hear faint sounds. Inside the room, Heaven saw Nevaeh, Devonte, and another woman engaged in a threesome.

"I guess I walked into some shit I wasn't supposed to."

They all looked up, startled.

Nevaeh jumped out of the bed. "Damn Heaven, I didn't know you were coming over tonight!"

"What up, Heaven? I never expected you to see me like this." Devonte's hard dick hung as he spoke.

"Trust me, I wasn't trying to."

Can you cover that thing up?

And you must be the trainer."

"I am! Damn, Nevaeh, you never told me you had a twin. Care to join?"

"Nah, she don't want to join. We not into that incest shit." Nevaeh said, jumping up, grabbing her robe, walking towards heaven.

"Let's go downstairs."

Downstairs, Nevaeh grabbed a bottle of wine and poured herself a glass. Heaven followed her and sat down on the sofa.

"Sorry, you had to walk in on that. I would've offered you some wine, but I see you have water. Anyways, why didn't you call first?"

"Nevaeh, what kind of freaky shit you on up in here. You got your ex-husband in the bed with your trainer. Dick just slinging. Yes, I'll take that glass of wine." Heaven grabbed a glass from the kitchen and passed it to Nevaeh.

"So, you went from having orgy's at Drelow's parties to threesomes now?"

"Sis, I'm grown and single and can do whatever I like. And that upstairs, I like. I'm in control of that dick and that clit." Nevaeh bit her bottom lip.

"Too much information," Heaven said, drinking down a big gulp of the wine.

"I did Drelow eyelashes, and she brought your costumes to the shop today but damn Heaven, I didn't know you were coming over here tonight to grab them. You could've called first. Anyways, your stuff is in the closet."

Heaven walked over to the closet and picked up the black clothing bags. She unzipped the bags and took the costumes out.

"This what I'm talking about," she said, impressed.

"That shit looks old to me." Nevaeh made a face at the long, frumpy dress heaven had pulled out. Heaven looked over the costumes before zipping the bags back up.

"I came to hang out with you and talk for a few, but I see you tied up."

"Perhaps you'll call next time, sis, instead of walking into my shit. Now, I have some body parts to get back to."

Nevaeh finished her wine and escorted Heaven to the door.

"Call me when you're not fucking."

The following day, Garrick called Heaven while she ate breakfast.

"Good morning, Garrick!" Heaven said, filling a coffee pot with bottled water.

"What up, partner! So, how do the costumes look?" Heaven took a bite of the strawberry cream cheese bagel.

"They look like we'll fit right in. I'm about to look at that TV show The Handmaid's Tale Drelow was telling me about. Just call me when you're on your way."

"Will do! I have to run a few errands real quick. I'll holla at you later."

"Okay!"

Brook sat on her Boca do Lobo couch in her spacious Living room, watching a SOAP OPERA on TV. Her doorbell rang, startling her Yorkie, who jumped off her lap. Brook walked to the front door, the dog on her heels. Garrick was at the door. "I'm here! So, what is it you need help with?"

Brook looked him up and down.

"Thanks for coming bye." She gestured for him to come in. "I won't hold you up long."

She walked into the kitchen, and Garrick followed her. The vast hallway was hung with expensive paintings, and Garrick looked around in amazement. "What a beautiful home you have."

"Thank You! Would you like something to drink? I made some punch. Will that be okay?"

"That will be fine."

Brook filled a glass with punch and handed it to Garrick. "I spoke with your partner Heaven, and she told me what's going on. I really hope this lead you guys have will lead me to my child."

"It's a good lead, Ma'am."

"Again, enough with the Ma'am stuff. Please, call me Brook."

"Brook, I believe we have a strong lead, and once we get onto the compound, we should know much more by then."

"That will be great! I have been waiting for this, it seems a lifetime."

She suddenly hugged Garrick, smiling. Then she released him and gestured for him to sit down at the island.

"Is that why you called me over, to talk to me about the case?

What's in this punch? It's good!" he said, drinking it up.

Brook smiled. "Herbs from my garden."

"Speaking of garden, my groundskeeper's wife went into labor, and he had to leave." She gestured for Garrick to walk over to the sliding doors, as they both walked out onto the patio. "Is it possible for you to finish what he started? I can pay you."

"I guess I can help if you give me some more of that punch. No need to pay me."

"No, I was paying the gardener, and I will pay you now to finish up where he left off."

She walked out onto the patio. "As you can see, there's the lawnmower. After filling the lawn bags with grass, you can place them in the garage. I'll bring you out more punch.

She went back inside, grabbing more punch, placing it on the patio table. I'll see you when you're done."

An hour later, a sweaty Garrick re-entered the house. "Brook? I'm done!" He called out.

Garrick went over to the master's bedroom door, where he could hear the shower running, and knocked.

"Brook, I'm done!"

"Come in!" Brook shouted through the door.

Inside, Brook was standing in the shower, Naked. Garrick looked at her body through the clear shower glass and swallowed.

"I see your all sweaty and dirty. Take them clothes off and join me."

"Join you! I wasn't expecting this. Are you sure?"

"I wouldn't have called you over if I wasn't."

Garrick peeled his sweaty clothes off and joined Brook in the shower. "Hmm, so is this the real reason you called me over?"

"Are you complaining about being here?"

"Not at all!"

Brook grabbed Garrick's dick and started massaging it in her hands.

They got out the shower, as Garrick carried Brook, laying her on the California King size bed. Brook positioned herself at the edge of the bed, spreading her legs to expose her pink pussy.

"Come give me some of that," she said seductively.

Garrick climbed on top of her, and she wrapped her legs around him. She grabbed a condom from under the pillow and unrolled it over Garrick's erect dick. Garrick slid into her and started thrusting. Brook dug her fingers into his back as he pounded her pussy.

"Shit, that dick feels good. Fuck me, Garrick. Fuck me!" She lifted her hips to meet Garrick's thrusts, each pump bringing her closer to the edge. Garrick pumped into her, and her moans became louder as she climaxed. He pushed into her one more time, and they both collapsed, lying there breathing heavily.

"Damn, that was good," Brook said, turning over to look into Garrick's eyes. "I guess that punch worked."

"Punch!"

"Yeah, the punch I gave you, it's a cannabis cocktail called rock hard I put together, and I see now where it gets its name from. It lives up to its expectations."

She rubbed his dick before putting it into her mouth. Garrick grabbed a fistful of her hair as he bobbed her head up and down onto his dick.

It wasn't long before he started breathing heavily and cumming intensely.

Chapter Seven

Heaven, Garrick, Detective Pratt, and a middle-aged man sat at the round table at the Spotlight Office, looking over surveillance photos. The man was Agent Charles.

"You two will come into the compound with Agent Charles and me. Garrick, you will be brought in as a bidder. Heaven, you will join the other women and I on the ground for the festivities," Pratt said. Bringing you guys in will not be a problem. I already informed Mr. Samuel's that I will be having visitors from out of town who would like to give a charitable donation to the compound."

"Heaven and I will roam the compound as Agent Charles, and Garrick look investigate what's happening inside Mr. Samuel's mansion. So, Garrick told me about the costumes you guys have. May I see them?" Pratt said, looking over at Heaven.

Heaven walked over to the sliding closet doors and took out the two black clothing bags she had picked up from Nevaeh's house. She unzipped the bags and placed them on the table. Garrick picked up his pants and sized them up, putting on the all-black two-button jacket.

"It feels like this costume was tailored for me."

"Yeah, Drelow said she sized you up and knew what exactly to put together for you," Heaven said.

"I bet!"

"Once we get in, we will join in on some festivities with Samuels and his wife. Afterward, we will break off, and that's when we will join the other men for the bids," Agent Charles said.

"So, tell us about these Bids?" Heaven asked.

"They bring young girls out, and men bid on them," Pratt said.

Garrick looked at her. "Once they bid, then what?"

"The girls are taken to an excluded area where there are different rooms. It's dark down there; mind you, there are guards securing every area," Agent Charles described.

"We need to get down there and take pictures of the girls being bidded on and the men who are bidding on them," said Pratt.

"And what about our assignment?" Heaven asked. "We still have to find the blond, greyed-eyed child, I mean man, and get some type of DNA for our client."

"You'll know Clay when you see him. Trust me!" Pratt told her.

Agent Charles pulled out a plastic Ziploc bag. He passed Heaven and Garrick ID cards. "Here are your IDs."

"We had these made for you," Pratt said.

Heaven took the ID cards from Agent Charles. "Good idea!"

"So, if they try to run these names, we should be all good?" Garrick asked, turning the card over in his hand.

"Yes, you'll be known as Mr. And Mrs. Lewis," said Pratt.

"Samuels will want to know more about you before letting you bid," Agent Charles said.

"You will come up as owners of an online dating site for those looking to meet and greet," Pratt said.

Heaven looked at Garrick and smirked. "We could pull this off."

"We got this! This not nothing new to us."

"What's the name of this dating service?" Heaven asked.

"Climax Dating Services," Agent Charles answered.

Heaven and Garrick exchanged looks and burst out laughing.

"I guess the title will do, considering what they got going on," said Heaven.

Agent Charles reached into his jacket pocket and passed Garrick a pair of glasses and Heaven, a red rose pendant.

"What are these for?" Garrick asked. Heaven examined the pendant. "This is cute," She said.

Garrick put on the glasses and looked in the mirror. "I can rock these with my fit."

"I'm glad you guys like them," said Agent Charles. "The glasses will record everything you look at, Garrick. Heaven, the rose is a camera as well, and both have audio too."

"Ok, now we on some real James Bond shit." Garrick stood posing with the glasses. They all laughed.

"So, we all good?" Pratt asked.

"Yeah, we're good to go," Garrick said.

"Great!" Agent Charles clapped his hands together. "We'll all meet here tomorrow morning and drive into the compound together."

Chapter Eight

The next morning, Heaven and Garrick were waiting in their office, dressed in their costumes. Garrick put on a pot of coffee while Heaven examined herself in the mirror. Agent Charles and Pratt walked in dressed up, similar to how Heaven and Garrick were dressed.

"Good morning, Detective Pratt and Agent Charles."

"You guys care for some coffee?" Garrick asked.

"Sure!" said Agent Charles. "I like it black."

Pratt moved in on the group. "You guys look nice in your costumes, and Drelow did a good job."

She looked at Garrick. "You're looking handsome over there too, Garrick."

"Thank you, Detective Pratt." Garrick passed Agent Charles a cup of coffee. "Detective Pratt, would you like a cup of coffee as well?"

"That will be nice. Do you remember how I like it?"

Heaven smirked. Yes, I do! Garrick poured two creams and two packs of sugar into the cup of coffee, stirred it up, and passed it to Pratt.

"Heaven, that pendant looks nice on you, and Garrick, the glasses bring the suit out as you stated." Agent Charles complimenting both Heaven and Garrick."

"The pendant and the glasses will record everything, sending the audio and video straight to our team," Pratt said.

Agent Charles turned to Garrick. "Garrick, remember, if asked why you're here, you can tell him I told you about the festivities, and you guys came for the entertainment."

Garrick nodded. "We got this! We've done plenty of undercover work. This will be a breeze."

"We have a rental. After the services, we will be heading to the compound," Agent Charles stated.

That afternoon, Church goers flocked out of the temple after the service. Mr. Samuel's, standing at the entrance of the building, smiled broadly and shook hands with everyone. Agent Charles approached him.

"Mr. Samuel's, as always, service was great."

"Ah, Peter! Glad to see you and your wife were able to make it."

"We wouldn't have missed this for the world." Agent Charles smiled. "These are my guests I spoke to you about." He turned to Heaven and Garrick, who was standing with him, wearing polite smiles. "This is Mr. David and Hanna Lewis."

"Nice to meet you. I'm glad you could join us for service today," Mr. Samuel's said. He shook Garrick's hand firmly and gave Heaven a nod and a soft handshake as well.

"It's finally nice to meet you, Mr. Samuel's. Peter speaks highly of you," Garrick spoke in a confident tone.

"Yes, and your service was great. I can imagine how great the festivities will be," Heaven added.

"Glad you all enjoyed! I'll be seeing you all at the compound, I suppose?"

"Yes, Sir!" Agent Charles replied. "We wouldn't miss it for the world.

We're on our way now."

They all walked off to the parking lot.

Agent Charles grabbed his cell phone inside his car and started dialing even before the others were buckled in.

"Did you get all that?" he said to the phone. "Great! We're on our way to the compound. After this, we should have all the evidence we need to indict Mr. Samuel's, the bidders, and his goons." He hung up the phone and drove off with a menacing smile.

"Agent Charles pulled up to the gate. He was approached by two of Mr. Samuel's Henchmen. Hi, I'm Peter, and we're here for Mr. Samuel's. The guard looked at peter as the other guard looked into the car. These are my guest for the festivities. Mr. Samuel's is aware," Agent Charles told the guard.

"The tall, muscle-bound guard spoke in a deep tone. Yeah, I know who you are. My boss informed us you guys were coming, but I still need to see IDs for whoever enters the compound grounds."

Garrick, Heaven, and Pratt all passed Agent Charles their IDs. Agent Charles passed the IDs to the guard, and the guard swiped the IDs through a reader and handed them back.

"You're all clear. Enjoy the festivities!"

The gates opened into the multi-acre compound, a labyrinth of homes, stores, businesses, and stables anchored by a massive mansion. As they engaged in the festivities, dozens of men, women, and children talked, laughed, and enjoyed food and drinks.

A dark-haired woman who looked to be in her thirties, looking like the Stepford Wives type, approached them with one of Mr. Sumuel's' henchmen. Garrick and Heaven braced themselves.

"I see you guys made it! Welcome!" she greeted them.

"These are our guests," Agent Charles said.

"Yes, my husband spoke of them. He informed me to escort you ladies onto the grounds to engage in the festivities as the guys join my husband and the other men in the mansion for drinks."

Garrick and Agent Charles followed the guard to the mansion with a bit of hesitation as Heaven and Pratt stayed with the woman. "You ladies can follow me. We have all types of festivities going on today."

Inside a sunroom, a group of women sat in rocking chairs, knitting and talking among themselves as Pratt, Heaven, and the dark-haired woman approached.

"We have guests! You all remember Mrs. Johnson, and this is her guest, umm--"

"I'm Mrs. Lewis," Heaven said. The ladies greeted them with friendly smiles.

"Please have a seat," the woman insisted. Pratt and Heaven sat down next to each other.

"Mrs. Lewis do you knit?" the woman asked Heaven.

"Yes! My grandmother taught me when I was rather young."

"Great! I'm aware that Mrs. Johnson can knit. You care to join us, Mrs. Lewis?"

"Sure!"

"Entertainment in thirty minutes. Until then, let's just talk, knit, and enjoy our cheese and wine."

Heaven asked, "You say entertainment. May I ask what type of entertainment?"

"We have performers and dancers and other activities going on too."

"Sounds like it will be fun," Heaven said.

"Now, Mrs. Lewis, what type of business do you and your husband have?" the woman asked. All the women in the room looked at Heaven, waiting on her to respond.

"We bring people together," Heaven said.

Mrs. Samuels raised her eyebrows curiously. "You bring people together?"

"Yes! My husband and I own a dating service." Heaven could hear the women mumbling to each other at her response.

"That sounds like an exciting business to be in," said Mrs. Samuels."

"It's a way for people to meet, the single and lonely," Heaven

mentioned.

"It's a really good site," Pratt joined in on the conversation. "Especially for those looking to meet new people and to have fun." She smiled and took a sip of the wine. The other ladies smiled politely and continued with their knitting.

In the expensive living room of Samuels Mansion, the warm afternoon sun filtered through the high windows as the men sat around, talking among themselves and enjoying cigars and cognac.

"You have a nice home, Mr. Samuel's," Garrick said. He sipped his drink and admired the furniture and shiny hardwood floors.

"Thank you, Mr. Lewis. I can imagine with the business you and your wife have, you have a lovely home too."

"I can't complain!"

Two men entered the room: a tall young man and an older gentleman who walked limp.

"Excuse me," Mr. Samuel's said to Garrick. "I see my other guest have arrived."

The two men walked towards Mr. Samuel's as he began to walk their way.

The younger, taller man wore a long trench coat, a three-piece all-black suit, a white shirt, and a leather top hat. The older man was dressed relatively the same, but his suit was a dark gray, and he wore a fedora hat.

Mr. Samuel's reached them and greeted them. "Hello, gentlemen! Glad to see you made it."

"Do we have any new bidders?" The older man asked.

"Yes, we have a few. The women are being entertained at the hall. Shall we begin?"

"Sure!"

Mr. Samuel's stepped into the middle of the room and spoke to everyone.

"Hello, gentlemen. Glad to see that you all could make it to our social gathering this year."

Garrick turned and whispered to Detective Charles. "Hmm, I see there are drinkers in the house. Didn't know these religious boys drink like this."

Agent Charles smirked. "Religious, my Ass! Some of them will drink you under the table. Remember not to drink too much and keep your eyes open."

"We have new entertainment this year that I believe you all would love. Grab your drinks and follow me," Mr. Samuel's said to the men.

The men followed Mr. Samuel's down some stairs leading to an underground bunker. Garrick saw that they had walked into a long corridor of individual mini-faux bedroom setups where young women in lingerie were posted up like a sex market display. The young naked women walked around as the guests leered at them.

"Now that you see what's available let's begin the bidding," Mr. Samuel's announced.

Garrick walked over to Agent Charles. Seeing those nubile women wearing nothing but lingerie made it difficult for his dick to stay in check. "I didn't know we'll be walking into something like this," he whispered to Agent Charles. "A house full of pussy...."

Garrick looked as excited as a kid in a candy shop.

"Tempting! Just make sure you're getting all this and keep your hands and dick to yourself," Agent Charles said. "Remember, some of these girls are underage."

Garrick looked across the room and saw a man who resembled Clay Moore. "That looks like the guy Pratt was telling us about."

"You're correct! That's Clay Moore."

"Hmm, show-time! I'm going to go talk to him and feel him out."

Garrick started walking towards Clay. As he approached, he overheard Clay talking to another guest.

"Yeah, she is fine," Garrick said.

Clay and the gentleman he was engaged in conversation with both looked up at Garrick.

"Yes, she is! Clay said I didn't catch your name as he looked at Garrick."

"I didn't throw it. Garrick begins to laugh. My name is Mr. Lewis."

"Oh, now that was funny. I walked right into that. Clay smiled! I'm Clay Moore, and this is Mr. Larkin." Garrick shook both their hands.

"Nice to meet you, gentlemen."

"So, where you from, Mr. Lewis?" Clay asked.

"I'm from Colorado and a guest of Peter's."

Garrick looked over at Agent Charles, who seemingly looked to be watching some of the girls.

"Oh, Peter! Yes, I know of him. Glad you were able to make it to the festivities."

"I'm glad I made it too."

Garrick looked around the room at the ladies and licked his lips.

"Peter invited you here, you say? You must have some deep pockets for him to do that. May I ask what type of work you do, Mr. Lewis?"

Garrick chuckled. "Work! People work for me."

"People work for you? So, I take it you own your own business," Clay said.

"You're Correct! I own a dating service."

"Hmm! Never met anyone who owned that type of business," Mr. Larkin said. "Excuse me, gentlemen, I'm going to grab another drink before the bidding starts." He walked off.

"A dating service! Interesting," Clay said. "Perhaps, you can try it out one day? We're online too."

Garrick passed Clay a Business Card. "Now, I wouldn't mind what's sitting behind display number five," he said, licking his lips again.

"I see we have the same taste."

"If you're talking about her right here..." Garrick stared at the young lady who walked towards them with a tray of drinks. "She could feel on this here any night."

The men grabbed a drink off the tray as the young lady walked by. Clay looked at Garrick as he watched the young lady walk away.

Garrick sipped his drink. "So, you say you know of Peter, Mr. Moore? Yes, I've seen him with Mr. Samuel's at the Temple a few times. Clay said as he sipped on his drink. So, do you golf? Garrick asked as he watched Clay's every move. I'm asking because one of the guys had to back out, and we need one more person to play partners. Care to join us?"

"Golf is my game. Where will you guys be teeing up at?

"We'll be playing at the Riviera Country Club."

"The Riviera! Hmm, only the rich and famous play there." How were you able to get in? Garrick chuckled! Let's just say my pockets run deep.

"How about you give me your number, and I'll call you tomorrow with the details." Garrick passed Clay his phone.

Clay put his number in Garrick's phone and passed it back. "I guess I'll polish up my golf clubs tonight," he said excitedly.

"I look forward to playing with you guys. I'll reach out to you in the morning."

Garrick turned around and walked back over to Agent Charles. Mr. Samuels was standing at a podium.

"Gentleman, Gentleman, we are ready to bid. Behind display number one, we have Mary Jo."

The young woman in display number one got up from her chair and exposed her naked body to the men.

"The bid starts at Five Hundred. Do I hear Five Hundred?"

"Five hundred!" One bidder shouted.

"Five-fifty!" shouted the second bidder.

"Seven!" someone shouted.

"I have Seven Hundred! Going once. Going twice." Mr. Samuel's hit the gavel. "Sold for Seven Hundred Dollars. Please join your gift behind display number one and enjoy, Mister."

"Wow, this some unbelievable shit here. Ass Straight being bid on," Garrick said.

"I'm looking forward to locking all their asses up." Agent Charles said as he looked at the girls and turned back towards Garrick. "These girls, some of them look my daughter's age. I'm locking their whole fucking crew up, bidders and all. We got all the evidence we need."

"Not to mention the glass Clay put down." Garrick opened his coat slightly to show Agent Charles the rock glass Clay had been drinking from, which he had stashed inside his pocket.

"The prints and DNA on this glass will help us with solving our client's case."

"That was slick, grabbing his glass for DNA. We have to put in a bid, though, so we won't look suspicious."

They both turned to look at Mr. Samuel's, who was still calling out bids.

"Do I hear four hundred?"

"Four-fifty!" Agent Charles Shouted, and Mr. Samuel's hit the Gavel.

"Sold to Mr. Johnson."

"You're really going to go in there with that young girl?" Garrick asked Agent Charles with a *what the fuck you doing face.*

"She may look young, but she's undercover too! By the way, you're to bid on girl number nine, and she's undercover too. They're part of our 21 young street crew." They're just as grown as you but look much younger.

"I see! So, since she's grown, can I smash?" I mean we can work and play at the same time.

No more drinks for you. Agent Charles shook his head as he walked off.

I was playing, dude. Have a sense of humor.

Chapter Nine

That night, Heaven, Garrick, Pratt, and Agent Charles arrived back at The Spotlight Office. Garrick opened a bottle of water.

"Anyone like a bottle of water?" he asked the group.

"I wouldn't mind a bottle," said Pratt.

"Me too!" Heaven said.

"Agent Charles?"

Agent Charles was on the phone but gestured that he would like a bottle too. Garrick grabbed four bottles of water and walked back to the round table. He passed them around and sat down. "Damn, I ain't never seen no shit like that before," Garrick said as he twisted the cap off the bottle of DRIP water and took a sip.

Heaven was curious to know what Garrick was talking about. "What happened? What did you see?"

"A lot."

Agent Charles finished making his call. "I just spoke with Agent Miguel, and he has the footage from the spy glasses and the rose pendant."

"Good!" Pratt said with excitement in her voice. "So, we're finally good to take Mr. Samuel's and his henchmen down?" Yes, we are! Agent Charles said as he sipped on his bottle of water. Man, y'all just don't know, this case here means a lot to me. Thank you for helping us with this, guys."

"We were glad to help, and I appreciate you and Agent Charles for inviting us into the compound to help us with our case as well," Heaven said.

"Speaking of case, I met Mr. Clay Moore," Garrick told Heaven.

"You met him?"

"Yes! And I must say, he looks just like our client. Blond hair and all."

"Great!"

"Not just that...." Garrick stood up and walked over to the coat rack, taking the rock glass from his jacket pocket. He held the glass with a napkin and displayed it for Heaven to see. I got his DNA right here, spit and all. Heaven smiled at Garrick. How did you manage to get the glass and with his DNA on it at that? Garrick chuckled! Let's just say I got a little close to him.

"I'm going to run this over to forensics and have them compare this DNA to the swap we had our client take."

"Good job Garrick! So, Agent Charles, what happens from here?" Heaven asked.

"I will take this information and the surveillance to the District Attorney, who will then begin putting together indictments for Mr. Samuel's, his bidders, and his goons."

"Again, we appreciate you guys helping us with this," Pratt said.

"No problem!" Garrick replied.

"Like my partner said, anytime.

Agent Charles and Pratt stood up and started walking towards the door to leave. Pratt turned around, looking at Garrick in a flirty way. "I'll see you around, Garrick." She walked out, getting into the car with Agent Charles.

"I'll see you around, Garrick!" What's all that about?" Heaven asked.

"Don't tell me you're jealous. Remember, you said to keep it professional between us."

She smirked. "You're right! It's none of my business."

The next morning, Heaven was awakened by her phone ringing.

"Garrick, do you know what time it is?" she said sleepily into the phone.

"It's a match! Clay is Brook's son."

Heaven sat up in the bed, wiping the eye boogers from her eyes.

"Yes! We need to call Brook first thing in the morning and let her know."

"I already did that. I called Clay too and told him to meet me at Brook's house."

"You did what!? Called Clay! So, he knows about Brook?"

"No! He thinks we're going to play some golf today, and I told him to meet me there so they can finally meet. He thinks he's meeting me at our guest house."

"Nice." Heaven smiled.

Chapter Ten

Brook sat on her patio with her two Grey Danes, eating a bagel and cream cheese with a cup of coffee. The doorbell rang, and Garrick and Heaven arrived at Brook's house.

"Good morning! Please come in. I'm sitting on the patio. Join me."

Brook headed towards the patio as Heaven and Garrick followed.

"What a beautiful house you have here, Brook," Heaven said.

Garrick smirked to himself as he had a flashback of fucking Brook. "Yes, what a beautiful house it is," he agreed.

They all sat at the patio table as the dogs played in the spacious backyard.

"Your Danes are beautiful," Heaven said as she looked at the dogs engage playfully.

"Thank you! So, Garrick called me last night and told me you guys found my son."

"The DNA test from the glass came back with a ninety-nine percent match," Garrick said.

You could hear the excitement and emotions in Brook's voice.

"And this is why Williams recommended me to you guys. A glass! How were you able to get a glass with his DNA?"

"Let's just say we had help on the inside," Garrick answered.

Heaven placed her hand on top of Brook's hand. "Are you ready to meet your son, Brook?"

"Yes, I'm more than ready. I have been waiting for this moment for years."

The doorbell rang.

"I'll get that," Garrick said as he stood up. I asked some of my detective friends to come over. Garrick walked to the front door opening it, and clay was standing there with a big ass smile on his face, holding his golf clubs.

"Good morning, Mr. Lewis." Garrick gestured for him to step in.

"Morning, Mr. Moore. I see you're ready to hit the course, and you've shined your clubs all up, too—nice clubs, by the way. Please follow me. I have someone I would like for you to meet that will be joining us." Garrick led clay towards the patio.

"Nice artwork! Kinda remind you of Mr. Samuel's paintings," Clay said, admiring the paintings that hung on the wall. They reached the Patio. Heaven and Brook stared at Clay.

"Ladies, this is my guest, Mr.

Clay Moore." Garrick gestures

for Clay to have a seat.

Hello, ladies!

Brook just stared at him.

"Hi, I'm Heaven, and this is--" Before Heaven could finish talking, Brook cut Heaven off and said to clay.

"You look just as I imagined! Tall, blond, and handsome."

"Hmm? Garrick, are you trying to add me to your dating service," Clay mumbled under his breath. I think she's a little too old for me.

Garrick looked at him. "Clay, we need to talk."

Clay looked puzzled. "Sure! What's going on? Are we still hitting the golf course?"

Brook begins to speak. "Clay, I don't know how to tell you this, but I'm your mother and I hired Garrick and Heaven to find you."

"Who's Garrick? And who the hell are you? And what do you mean you're my mother?" Clay looked confused.

"Clay, this is my partner Heaven and my name is Garrick, not Mr. Lewis. We're private investigators and do not own a dating service but a Private Investigator business. As the lady said, we were hired to find you."

"What do you mean, you were hired to find me? Find me for what? I wasn't lost." Turning to Brook, he said, "And what's this bullshit about you being my mother?"

"Watch your mouth son, we have ladies present. Garrick said. Clay, she's telling the truth. Brook is your mother," Heaven Spoke in a calming voice.

"Brook? My mother!?" He stood up, looking at the three of them. Brook stood up too.

"My name is Brook, and I'm your birth mother."

"My mother? No, my mother's name is Elizabeth. What is this, a fucking joke?"

Clay looked over at Garrick, then back to Brook.

"That lady you know as Elizabeth is not your mother. I had you when I was very young, and you were taken away from me."

"Taken from you!?"

"Yes!"

"I'm a grown man. If any of this is true, why in the hell have you waited all this time to come looking for me now?"

When Brook spoke, her voice cracked. "I was scared."

"Scared of what?"

"I was scared to go back."

"Again, scared of what? And scared to go back where? I'm not going to ask you again, lady."

Clay's breathing had gotten heavier.

"Don't call me "lady." My name is Brook, and I was scared to come looking for you out of fear that I'll be beaten."

"Beating? Beat by who?"

Brook did not respond.

"I don't know what's going on, but I do know I do not have time for this here." Clay picked up his golf clubs and began to walk towards the patio doors.

"I was scared to go back because of my father."

Clay turned around. "Your father?"

Heaven stood up and walked over to Brook, rubbing her back to comfort her. Brook struggled to find words.

"Breathe!" Heaven said to her. Brook took in a deep breath and exhaled. "I'm okay! It's time for the truth to be told."

"I was scared to come looking for you because I was banned from my father's home. I was hurt and felt ashamed." Tears fell down Brook's face. "I was ashamed that my father got me pregnant."

"Got you pregnant? What do you mean, your father got you pregnant? If this story you're telling me is true, are you saying your father is my father?"

"Look, listen, man, she's telling the truth," Garrick said.

"This can't be true. My mother's name is Elizabeth Moore, and my father is Ammon Moore."

Garrick reached into his jacket pocket and pulled out an envelope. He passed it to Clay. Clay opened the envelope. He glanced at it, looked at Brook, and then back at Garrick.

"DNA results? How in the hell did you get my DNA?"

"At the bidding when you set your glass down," Garrick said.

"So, you're saying my parents aren't my parents, and my whole life has been a freaking lie?"

Brook asked the following question with some hesitation. "What is your father's name?"

Clay stared at Brook, distressed.

"His name is Cedar. Cedar Smith."

"Mr. Cedar Smith. I knew of him when I was younger. He and my dad were friends before he died, and I remember going to his funeral." Clay starts to pace the patio slowly with disbelief on his face.

"You mean to tell me the man I've known as my father's friend was my father?"

"Yes, and there's more," Garrick said.

Clay continued to pace the patio as he stared at Brook. "What more can there be?"

"Mr. Samuel's compound has been under investigation for running a prostitution ring and other illegal activities," Garrick explains. Clay's eyes widened.

"As my partner said, the compound has been under investigation for quite some time. Indictments will be given to those involved."

Clay broke out in a sweat.

"I have nothing to do with a prostitution ring or anything else that goes on at that compound."

"But we have you on surveillance at these biddings, as Mr. Samuel's calls them," Garrick said.

"I was only at the compound because I drove my dad. And yes, you've seen me at the biddings because I've been seeing one of the young ladies that work there.

"Oh, I take it you're referring to the woman, or should I say the tray girl at the bidding. You straight fucking the bottle, girl. I'm not mad at you because she is fine, and you're lucky she's grown," Garrick said.

Clay leaned against the patio railing, absorbing everything that had been said.

"Back to what I was saying, we also know about your dad, or should I say, Mr. Moore?"

"I don't believe this. My parents aren't my parents. My cousins, aunts, and uncles, their not my blood. So, my whole life, I've been lied to."

The three could see that clay was anguished. "Seriously! You bought me here to tell me I'm a fucking child of incest," Clay spoke loudly, staring at Garrick and Brook. Excuse my language!

Brook started walking up to Clay. "I'm sorry!" she said to him. I was young, and I couldn't stop him. "There was nothing I could do." You could see Clay's eyes watering up.

The Doorbell rang.

"I'll get that!" Garrick said, walking into Brook's house and returning with Agent Charles and Pratt.

"Clay, this is FBI Agent Charles and Detective Pratt."

"Hmm! Agent Charles. I thought your name was Peter. I've seen you at the Temple a few times, but we weren't formally introduced," Clay said.

"No, need for introductions then. But we'll tell you why we're here now," Agent Charles responded.

"Now that we've been formally introduced, we're here to ask you to testify against Mr. Samuel's, his bidders, and also against your parents or, should I say, Mr. and Mrs. Moore, Pratt said."

"Testify? Now, why would I want to do that? My parents, they're all I've ever known and have. Mr. Samuel's, he's always been like an uncle to me. Now, why would I want to hurt the people I loved all my life."

"Because we have you on surveillance attending these biddings. This is Prostitution, Sex Trafficking, and Child Pornography. Not to mention buying a child. That's enough to throw you all under the jail," Agent Charles said furiously.

"Wait, I have nothing to do with what goes on at Mr. Samuel's place. I'm not a part of that," Clay said as he started to pace the patio again. Wow, here it is, I find out I have another mother, and you're sitting here telling me that I also have to turn in the only parents I've ever known? I'll need some time to think about this." To take this all in.

"We didn't ask you if you needed some time," Pratt said. "You even testify, or you're going down with them."

Agent Charles jumped in.

The compound is being raided as we speak.

"The Moore's have been arrested too."

Agent Charles displayed his handcuffs. "Are you going to testify, or should I cuff you now?"

Brook stepped up to Clay. "Look, I know this is a lot to take in, but you're my son, not the Moore's. Elizabeth, she could not have children, so my father sold you to them. The Moore's bought you from my father. Do the right thing, son. Testify! They are not your parents, and that Samuel man is not your uncle. He's a trafficker that pimps out young girls, Pratt said with a bitter voice."

"You'll be granted full immunity too for testifying," Agent Charles interrupted. "You can begin a new life with your real mother. The lady standing before you, whose blood is running through your veins."

Clay stood there for a minute, quietly contemplating. "I can't believe this here. It's more than a lot to take in. Just tell me what I'll need to do. I don't want to go to jail."

Chapter Eleven

A crowd of reporters swarmed around the compound as the Feds raided the place. The news media were excitedly reporting the mass- arrest live. Mr. Samuel's, Mr. Samuel's wife, and several of Mr. Samuel's henchmen were escorted into the waiting police vehicles.

Inside a courtroom, Clay sat on the witness stand.

"Can you tell the court who was the head of this prostitution ring?" the prosecutor asked Clay.

"Mr. Samuel's, "Clay responded.

"And how did you know about this prostitution ring?"

"I would take my father there on a few occasions, or should I say, the man who I thought was my father."

"And can you tell me what went on at Mr. Samuel's place?"

"He threw parties. Special parties."

"Did these parties consist of young women being auctioned off to men?"

"Yes!"

"So, what happens after someone wins the bid for one of the women, or should I remind the court underage girls were being bid on too?"

"They will go into a private room Clay said."

"Have you ever gone into a room with one of these women?"

"No! I just bought my father over at times. As I said, he and Mr. Samuel's were close friends. I'm not into young girls. They're not my type. Plus, I was seeing someone at the time."

"Yeah, we've heard. The bottle girl."

The prosecutor looked over at the bottle girl who sat at one of the courtroom benches.

Chapter Twelve

Clay and Brook sat on Brook's patio. It was a warm, sunny afternoon, and clay was playing with the Great Danes, who seemed to have taken a liking to him. Brook watched Clay play with the dogs and smiled.

"I'm so glad I found you. We have so much to talk about and catching up to do."

"Yeah, regardless of how my life was just turned upside down, I'm glad you finally had the courage to look for me and to tell me the truth, mother."

And, I'm glad you also had the courage, to tell the truth in court and put those away who were treating them women like that.

"Yeah, me too! Clay sipped on his wine. I must admit, people will be able to tell you're my mom."

Brook smiled. "I suppose you're right about that. You look just like me. Hair and all."

They both smiled.

"I arranged for our first outing together," Brook said excitedly, standing up.

"An outing? Hmm, I'm up to that. So, where are we going, Mother?" A big smile crossed Brook's face as she heard the word Mother come out of Clay's mouth.

"To get you some real clothes."

They both began to laugh as Brook grabbed Clay's arm, walking towards the garage.

At the Spotlight Office, Garrick stood at the coffee station making coffee. Heaven scrolled through her computer. "So, when were you going to tell me you were fucking our client?" She asked.

"Huh! What?"

"Don't huh what me. You don't have to play dumb. Remember, we have trackers on each other's phones in case of emergencies."

"Wow! I forgot all about that." Garrick pulled out his phone and began fumbling with it. "And you say I'm nosy. But if you must know, I'm digging her. She's different!"

"You digging her, or you digging that cougar ASS?"

Heaven laughed softly. Her cell phone rang.

"Somebody on some jealous shit, I see." Garrick begins to sing Jealous Girl by New Edition.

"Boy, you wish!" Heaven responded before she picked up her phone. "Hey, sis, what's going on."

Garrick walked back to his desk, sipping his coffee.

"Heaven, I'm glad you answered your phone. I need your help."

Nevaeh began to cry frantically into the phone.

"Nevaeh, what's wrong? What's wrong, Nevaeh? Did someone hurt you? Is the dog, okay?"

"No! I'm not hurt, and the dog is ok, but I'm at the police station. Someone killed Devonte, and they think I did it. They read me my fucking rights and everything."

"What do you mean, Killed Devonte? Devonte's dead?"

Garrick looked up with a concerned look on his face.

"What police station are you at."

"Your old precinct."

"We're on our way."

To be Continued...

Please feel free to enjoy other books/audibles by Tanya Hilson

Back Porch Neighbors (Play)

Back Porch Secrets (Urban Drama)

Ruby's Diner (Urban Drama)

Shadow Eyes (Crime Drama)

Shadow Eyes 2 (Crime Drama)

Human Collateral (Crime Drama)

John's Hidden Truth (Children Book)

My Cousin Sue (Children Book)

www.ingramcontent.com/pod-product-compliance
Lightning Source LLC
Chambersburg PA
CBHW072015170626
46813CB00005B/2153